Rap
With
Ten Thousand
Carabaos
In the Dark

Rappin'
With
Ten Thousand
Carabaos
In the Dark

Poems by Al Robles

UCLA Asian American Studies Center
Los Angeles

First Edition, February 1996

ISBN 0-934052-25-5 (Soft)

Book Design: Charlene Narita
Production: Darryl Mar
Cover Photo: Alan Kikuchi

UCLA Asian American Studies Center
3230 Campbell Hall
Los Angeles, CA. 90095

For my mother, Etang, my father, "Bulldog,"
and for the manongs and manangs

Acknowledgments

THERE SEEMS TO BE a beautiful relationship between poets and the northern rivers that all seems to flow through the same course. The relationship, in a sense, is responsible for this work. I am indebted to all the poets who have influenced me. To those beautiful children at the South of Market Center in San Francisco where I teach a poetry workshop; I owe them my gratitude, if not my whole heart and mind, for teaching me how to be more playful in everyday life.

My deepest appreciation is to my family: Etang, my mother, and of course to my sisters Shirley and Virginia and all my brothers: Anthony, Ray, Jimmy, Remy, Hansel, Tony, and David. My brother Russell was in a way the soul and spirit of the poems. Jimmy taught me how to read poems in the rain forest of Hawaii. And I am ever so thankful to Tais for passing on to me those rare poetical gifts. And to Jade, my niece, writing poems together in the early morning was an experience that has become part of my discipline. Anthony taught me how to read poetry in wood; Ray taught me how to read mountain dreams. My sister Teresa, told me: "Work on the manuscript." Fredda worked along with me in the poetry workshop, along with Alana the poet.

To many individuals, I give thanks: Luis Syquia, Norman Jayo, Jeff Tagami, Shirley Ancheta, Presco Tabios, Jamie Jacinto, Elsa E'der, Virginia Cerenio, Catalina Cariaga, Janice Mirikitani, Jessica Hagedorn, Nancy Hom, Doug Yamamoto, Richard Oyama, Oscar Penaranda, Orvy Jundis, Tony Remington, Kitty Tsui, Jocelyn Ignacio, Utopia, and many, many others. I owe a great debt to N.V.M. Gonzalez for his encouragement. My special thanks to the Kearny Street Workshop for their support over the years.

I would like to thank Russell Leong, the editor of UCLA's *Amerasia Journal,* for his invaluable suggestions and patience in editing my book and obtaining funding for it. His love of poetry made things easier: "Let your children go," he said.

Finally, I wish to thank Mee Har Tom, who lived each day as the poems came to life. She was the heart and soul of this book. Without her this book would never have happened.

Preface

ONE MOIST SUMMER MORNING in Watsonville, California, Al
Robles, Luis Syquia and I were walking alongside the strawberry
fields. The air smelled of fruit waiting to be picked. After picking a
few strawberries off the vine to eat, Al told us this story: "Some
Pilipinos asked me what part of the Philippines I came from. And I
told them Jackson and Kearny Streets. And they said 'Where's that?'
And I said, 'Close to Ifugao Mountain.' They turned away, still puz-
zled."

And so the mystery and history, the struggle and promise of
becoming a Pilipino in America can be found in the poetry of Al
Robles--oral historian, artist and community poet. Perhaps no one
has listened as closely to the voices of the Pilipino American com-
munity during the last thirty years, painstakingly recording the sto-
ries of first-generation Pilipino manongs who immigrated to Hawaii
and to the Western United States. In his creative work, Al has
reclaimed a community history for us all—Pilipino, Chinese,
Japanese, and new immigrant alike. His community, though mainly
Pilipino American, is inclusive. His poetry is inhabited by farm
laborers, factory workers, Zen monks, pool hustlers, cooks, chil-
dren, lovers, gamblers, preachers, warriors, pimps, prostitutes,
young bloods, musicians, tricksters, barbers, stray Buddhas and
goddesses. To each, he has given a blue note, a lyric refrain and a
promise to remember.

To share his poems with others, Al Robles has kindly granted
the UCLA Asian American Studies Center permission to publish this
volume of poetry, selected from hundreds written during the past
twenty-five years.

The following individuals assisted on the volume, for which we
are grateful: Mee Har Tom, for helping us in selecting the poems;
Sharon Park for typing the manuscript into the computer; Celine
Parrenas for proofreading; and Charlene Narita for designing the
book. Mary Kao designed the cover. Funding was provided partially
by the California Council for the Humanities and the Pangarap
Filipino American Literature Spring Forums (1992), the Rockefeller
Foundation American Generations Humanities Program (1990-
1993), and the UCLA Asian American Studies Center (1995).

Russell Leong
Editor, *Amerasia Journal*

Contents

III. CHINATOWN BLUES FOR BLUES POETS

As a Poet

FOR YEARS I'VE BEEN preparing koicha, a special kind of pow-
dered green tea, the color of winter moss. Built tea houses and
tea rooms. Laid down rocks from the northern rivers as far as the
Rogue River Wilderness. Lived from tea house to tea house writ-
ing poems with Konnyaku, a cat.

I was with the Kearny Street Writers' Workshop from way
back. Collected the stories and tales of the old manongs. As a
poet I've followed the footprints of the manongs. I gathered up
their history from Agbayani Village to Stockton, in the farms and
fields that stretched north, south, east and west. I followed them
deep inside fish bellies swimming across the icy cold Pacific
waters. Sat down with every single manong and watched as they
weaved out dreams from fishnets beneath trees, in the Kauai
rains. I cried out to them across the sugarcane fields. Mudfish cut
through my mind: manong–manong–manong–manong. The rain
pounded my mind and heart still.

"Who are you?" they asked. I cried out, "I am your son, your
nephew—lost in the mist of a thousand floating ifugao dreams."
Coconuts fell from the sky. Suddenly everything was still and
quiet. The rain ran down manong Carbonel's brown face. "Where
do you live?" I asked. He pointed to an old beat-up shack in the
back. I entered his weathered shack filled with dirt. A sack of rice
on the floor. Frozen fish toppled from the ice box. A big jar of
mountain-moss bagoong in the corner. I carried the jar outside in
the heavy rains. The rain passed through the fishnet like endless
tales of the past.

Then suddenly everything disappeared—the manong, the
trees, the shack, the jar of bagoong, the fishnet, the sugarcane
fields, the rains. Then everything returned. The manong was a
manong again. Everything was clear and everything returned to
the way it was. I could hear the rains. Everything was different
but the same.

Al Robles
August 6, 1995

I
Tagatac
In
Ifugao
Mountain

Tagatac in Ifugao Mountain

I traveled far back into the past
searching for ifugao mountain tribe
All the things I've learned
I threw out of my mind
All the books I've read
were not worth one roll
of toilet paper

Many long tales have been told
about ifugao mountain
All the stories I've heard
have not been written down

Who's going to travel
far back into the past?
Writing empty poems
to the wind
is closer to ifugao mountain
Brings the mind closer
to its roots

Crazy tales say
no path leads up or down
to ifugao mountain
A hundred thousand monkeys
hold the mountain strong

Turning back a thousand years
will bring you nowhere
Pushing the mind toward
ifugao mountain
is a waste of time
No one I know

ever made it there
and back

A Pilipino fisherman once said
that looking for your roots
will get you all tangled up
with the dead past
Don't fool around
with all that nonsense
Just keep quiet
Shut your mouth
Catch some fish

When Tagatac catches
a wild mountain goat
he jumps on its back
and rides it hard
until the goat drops
then gets it drunk
on ifugao wine
then he bites it hard
round the throat. Blood spurts
all over him
then he throws the goat
over the fire
until its belly swells up
then he cuts it wide open
Pulls on the entrails
wraps it round his body
then digs into it raw.

Tagatac says
that to eat raw goat is
pure pilipino
To eat with your hands
is to be free

and return back to your
ancestral roots
To drink goat's blood
sucking it from its throat
is to feel the veins
of the whole universe in
your body.

What stupid ass stories!
Who would believe in such tales!
Yet, if you were asked,
"What is the most important thing
in the world, the head or tail of a fish?
What would you answer?"
No matter what answer you give
it will be wrong
Those who tread the carabao's tail
do not speak

Down below
an old ifugao hunter
chased me behind some trees
"What are you doing there?"
he said.
"Who are you hiding from?"

"I'm looking for Tagatac
in ifugao mountain
who scribbles poetry
on rocks and trees"

"Where could I find
that son-of-a-bitch?"

The old ifugao hunter
looked up at me
and said nothing

Then he said,
"Do you like pig ears?"

Then he kept chewing
on the pig's ear
until the saliva ran down
the side of his mouth

The old ifugao hunter said,
"Tagatac doesn't come down
from ifugao mountain
There is nothing
he could tell you anyway
He speaks a weird tongue
Not many understand him

He has a filthy mind and body
and bathes in monkey urine
and carabao dung
and drinks goats' blood
Chews the eyes of wild boar.

Spends all his time
drinking ifugao wine
Drunk as a mountain fool
Writes poetry
in goat's blood."

The mind shouldn't bother
with the roots so much
If the mind bothers
with the roots
It'll forget
all about the weeds

Roots sprout up all over
like wild locust
Who is to say the weeds
are not the roots?
Who is to say the roots
are not the weeds?

When the weeds are all eaten up
the spirit grows deep
and when the spirit grows deep
the weeds spread far
and the roots grow strong

Even at the edge of a cliff
weeds grow high and wide
Nothing stops them from shooting up
Even in the ghetto the roots spread

Traveled many years
searching for ifugao mountain
Found nothing
but a dead path
leading nowhere
but inside a hole
full of pig shit

Surrounded by howling
ifugao head hunters
Leaped up high
over their heads
Threw pig shit in their faces
Then ran my ass
off a steep cliff

Looking for Tagatac
in ifugao mountain

is dangerous
You could get yourself killed

In the pool hall an old manong
will bend slowly and aim
and say "in that pocket
over there"
and know by the sound
if the cue ball goes in or not

There is only one sound
that comes from ifugao mountain
Tagatac says that it tells you
all you need to know
An ifugao mountain nose-flute sound
tells no lies.

A Thousand Pilipino Songs:
Ako Ay Pilipino

ako ay pilipino—from across the 7000 islands & seas
i am the blood-earth patis flowing thru the mountain
soil-veins of my people—the slated dung tongues of
winter rain mud-carabao—ako ay pilipino—i am pilipino—
the thousand-year-old savage-green moss-forest
ifugao bagoong—the sharp baguio wind piercing naked
igorat bodies—isda from the mindanao sea—
ako ay pilipino—i am the slated pink salmon from alaska
barreled in thick seasoned wood—floating around like
orange-persimmon buttocks fermenting in a bursting
semen-sky— isda clinging to the pounding waves—
slashing across like a bolo—drifting down to the bay of
san francisco—wading thru the thick soggy fog & down
the seaweed rocky shores—ako ay pilipino—i am pilipino
living out in the mission & manilatown & chinatown &
japantown & in central city & stockton & vallejo & salinas
& seattle & watsonville & san jose & hayward & mt. eden &
centerville & sacramento & isleton & walnut grove & up &
down the coast & on mountains & hills & below trees & near
rivers & streams & oceans & in the delano fields of brown
volcanic-breasts growing out of igorata nipa hut panao-
minds—ako ay pilipino—i am pilipino in a graveyard of
wallowing shrunken negrito heads—round savage faces—
hard rock-winter ancient bodies—with thick mango lips
sucking up tuba juice from carabao eyes—ako ay pilipino—
i am pilipino—manila cafe—san miguel—one thousand
drunken nights watching worn white silk whores trampling
their bodies on a ten-cent lacquered counter—
ako ay pilipino—i am pilipino—young & old—waiting for a
new day to rise—to raise my bolo—to slash down—to hack
the chain that binds my pilipino brothers and sisters—
ako ay pilipino—i am pilipino pain excreting dead blood of

pilipino poverty-minds—ako ay pilipino—i am pilipino
i am kearny street & the brown feet of manongs [immigrants] treading
pool hall dreams—empty pockets of echoing sadness in the
pit of lonely carabao bellies—i am international—st. paul—
shasta royal hotel tomato sardines under warm mattresses—
ako ay pilipino—i am pilipino—saturday nights at the pilipino
center—brown hands holding the young pinays [philipinas]—dancing to
tino's music: "come to me my melancholy baby, come to me
and i'll be true"—to your adobo skin—dancing to the rhythm
of the night—ako ay pilipino—i am pilipino—slick black hair
combed straight back with a little wave to catch the pinay's
eye—perfumed with nelson's pomade—the florsheim shoes
polished reflecting the pinay's pompadour—ako ay pilipino—
i am pilipino—on the dance floor with black-gray pinstripe
suits stretched out slick & cool—ako ay pilipino—dimas
alang—at the christening adobo & pansit & isda—lick the
lemon on the fish & kapatid of loin cloth pilipinos in the
sacramento river rice-shacks—in central city—bayanihan—
bayanihan—bayanihan—ako ay pilipino—i am pilipino—
kain [to eat] with your bare hands—feel the steaming hot kanin [cooked rice]
warming up then squeeze the tomatoes like blood in your
hands mix the chili peppers with onions & shoyu—eat fish
tails & fish heads & fish eyes & fish eggs—kumain [eating] all day
with a thousand pilipino suns in your belly, with the flame in
your tongue, with the flame in your eyes burning the sky rag-
ing—red—ako ay pilipino—i am pilipino—
dance wild into the dark night with cracking bamboo flute
sounds—dance until the roots in the ground grow strong
dance to ancient ways with spears & bolos & bamboo under-
wear—dance to the thunder throbbing wailing naked brown
bodies wrapped in wet banana leaves—dance to the poor
peasants dance to the wild ifugao dung-moon-smeared
women—dance to the flowing blood of wild pigs, spilling
down from the minds of pilipinos—dance to autumn-goats'
intestines—to the erection of a thousand pig ears & pig eyes
& pig heads & dance to don carlos carvajal & legaspi—kearny

street poet & worker for the pilipinos—dance to carlos
bulosan, pilipino poet—dance to carlos villa & leo valledor &
sid valledor & serafino malay syquia & all the manongs & to
pilipino faces in the jungles, in the cities, in the ghettos—
dance to carabao smells & fleas & seasons & tae—dance to
magsaysay—dance to my tatay^(father)—pilipino clown—gambler—
wild boar running wild in the pool halls, in the cities—
fisherman in alaska & fruit picker in stockton & a pilipino who
sang a thousand songs to his children ako ay pilipino—
i am pilipino—goddamn it!—ako ay pilipino—
dance to my tatay who pained and died each day—the blood
in his body drained out his eyes, his face, his heart & stomach
& brain & pulled my tatay into a fish-like grave smothered him
with red blazing chili peppers and tomatoes of the earth—
dance to my tatay who stood in the cold streets of chinatown,
in the rain holding onto a telephone pole—reaching for the
sun, a child's face, a hand to spring flowers in his dying
brain—dance to my tatay who loved life & ulam & chunks of
a mountain baboy—dance to my tatay with fish and rice in his
mouth—dance to the burning castration of magellan & iron
crosses pushing down pilipino faces & minds & bodies—
dance to cock fights & to the gods of the seas & skies &
mountains—dance to pregnant ifugao spirits—dance to the
manongs chasing 7th street blondies—dance to the faces &
eyes & feet of pilipino children—dance to their spirit that
swirls round a thousand rice fields & playgrounds & alleyways
in central city—dance to the clapping of brown hands & the
stomping of ancient feet & the snapping of forest-fingers—
dance to bill sorro & emil deguzman of the international
hotel—dance to tino's barbershop—dance to manong camara
& manong osas dance to etang, etang, etang stroking my hair
filled with carabao tae—dance to my nanay in the pilipino
sky—dance to the pilipinos struggling in the cities & farms
of america—ako ay pilipino—I am pilipino

Pilipino workers, Delano, California 1930

Agbayani Village

agbayani village
in the summer
the roosters cry out
this year
I saw manong taay
caressing his fighting cock
next year
when the rain falls
I'll be there too
when the rain water touches my face
I'll sing a hundred songs to the manongs
& a large fish will be cooking inside
ah, I've waiting a long time for this day
should I prepare for a long stay?
I didn't come to agbayani village
to keep silent
agbayani village is not too far away
from song or dance
even the roosters sing out
so how can agbayani village tales
tell you anything?
if you don't talk to delano carabaos
why one was buried the other day
ploughed the grape fields around the clock
and died very young
"but we celebrate his death
they'll celebrate mine, too . . .
when I die," says manong cardac.

International Hotel Night Watch

Carabao
I ride your thick hide
It smells of northern luzon fleas
The manilatown-kearny street wind
cuts thru thin blankets of the manongs
Chilled ifugao bones crack the lucky M cue ball

I listen to the long manong tales:

"Nobody could take care of the carabao
Some poor man take care in the mountains
So right now maybe I got plenty of carabao
My brother, kapatid
My sister got plenty of carabao
High price animal, boy!
You cannot kill the carabao when it's well
Otherwise you going to be punished by the law
You could kill the carabao when it is lame or cripple
If it cannot work no more
You could eat it
You could kill the cow anytime
But the carabao, no.
It takes long time. . . the carabao lives long time
About seven years old all teeth fall out
Then change new one
When no more new one they die
They cannot work no more
It's good eating
It takes two to five hours for carabao adobo
It's better than pig
Some carabao he lay down then you ride it
He lets you on his back

He's nice one, you know
Carabao is nice to you
When you come in the afternoon from the ricefield
He go home too, by himself
After the sun go down he lay down
Goddam! like a human being.
International Hotel Night Watch
Manong-carabao
I ride you thru the I-Hotel ricefields
One by one the carabao plows deep.

let the mabalian spirit tread around
the i-hotel rice fields
and pregnant nuns

swallow seven stars
manong
the clearings on the mountain
slope is ready, and cogon grass
is thick round your body

it's time now for me to cut the grass
around your body

trap wild pigs
lay down your bolo in a basket of rice
squat on the floor
balance your mind on heels
listen to the tinkling of bells
and of brass amulets, and the beating
of gongs.

pour coconut oil over your hair
rub down the body hard

pin-stripe macintosh suits
cling to hot savage bodies

rise up on heels and toes
bend the knees
twist the body encircling the gongs
dance around the small rooms

Manong Federico Delos Reyes
and His Golden Banjo

back home
in the p.i.
i ride the snake
i ride the monkey
i ride the waterbuffalo
i ride the lizard
i ride the fish
i ride the coconut tree
in america
i ride the southern pacific boxcar
montana snow-bound cries
shuffling brown feet
in centerville taxi dance halls
i chase after the white women
in manilatown
i ride the bar stool
at blanco's bar
scotch on the rocks express
dreaming of dark brown pinays
i ride the seven seas
1920 golden banjo
strumming
songs of romance

"yes sir—that's my baby
no sir—i don't mean maybe
yes sir—that's my baby doll."

silver wing cafe
"oh mama!

difficulty of surviving in America

you got my fishhead?
and two plates of rice. . ."

oh god, how i love my fishhead!
oh god, how i love my women!
oh god, how i love my music!

Manong Jacinto Santo Tomas

when the first sound of the
carabao is heard—all is clear
like pearls in the bottom of
the badjao sea.

"o'y o'y. come help me. hold dat one.
hang and dry dat fish in my room. first
i soak it in vinegar and salt. i cut from
da head down. spread like bird wings. if you
got plenty of dat one you lay dem flat inside
bathtub. da others you hang with dat rope."

"why i no can do dat?
who tell me like dat?
those people who eat with dat fork."

smile
manong jacinto
you gave
your
black thumb
to the rice gods
(who cares looking at the stars now, when you
can swallow each one).

manong
pound
the kulintang
rise up
in
your
cagayan loincloth
eat with carabao-winter hands

"why i got these for—my hands?
who give them to me?
the rice and fish taste better dat way."

Manong Camara

florin shadows
cross
my path
your old hat
can't keep
your eyes
from hiding
the balikbayan sun
manong
why don't you
& frederico
get together
your music
will bring carabao
closer together
esquire hotel blondies
left a long time ago
manong camara
you lived
a carabao's life
smoking manilatown cigars
in the northern luzon wind
p.i. cafe
the blondies breasts
sticks
like biko
five dollars
white flesh
inside your
macintosh zip
manong
what can you sing now?

" . . . for you
maybe i'm a fool—ah,
but it's fun people say
you rule me with one. . . wave
of your hand. baby it's grand.
they just don't understand—
living for you is easy living.
it's so easy to live when you're
in love. . . "

Benito Milliano,
the Rice Cake Manong

a yellow river full of saliva   *lives in his past*
damns up his hollow chest
like fish bones

"i don't know why i have too
much yellow saliva." manong
milliano spits out hot yellow
steam into the cold, foggy air:
a thin, shaking coconut tree.
moves like an old igorot
hangs onto my arm—fragile
bones. bows to the old women
on the street. . . winks at
the young ones. after a long rain
rice cake and tea clear the eyes

                  sword
a sharp kris
cuts the sky
in half—
fallen rice cakes!

who cares the winter
who cares the autumn
who cares the spring
who cares the summer

when i could swim the sacramento river
with twenty pounds of salmon on my back
you hear my kababayans calling:
milliano–milliano–milliano–milliano

Uncle Victor,
the Forgotten Manong

wobbles around freely
in the sacramento fields
lives in a run-down shack
tilts to one side
damp and cold
two empty rooms
a dirt floor
old weathered rags
dangle from a rusty nail
wind and rain
seep thru cracks
nothing grows
in the fields
only a few onions
uncle victor
eighty-five-year-old manong
still hanging around
from the old days
two old friends come by
on sundays
drinking up a gallon of wine
laughing loud and crazy
three drunk spirits
laid out flat
on their brown faces
field rats run in and
out of the kitchen
carrying off a whole loaf
of jewish rye bread

Manong Felix

dear manong felix
when i see
your brown face
i see
the rain forest
of my people
before white man's history
the luzon mountain landscape
clears my mind
in the deep crevasses
of your ancient face
the pasig river flows
in agbayani village
your family
was celebrating
your life
manong felix
i see
my tatay *father*
& nanay *mother*
& ninong *godfather*
& ninang *godmother*
& anak *child*
& kapatid *brother/sister*
& lolo *grandfather*
& lola *grandmother*
in you
the chicken adobo
smells good
i can taste
the thick adobo-tales
of your life

Manong felix brings the connection to the speaker's past and family

inside
your small room
the rice is cooked
your mata *eye*
catches mine
like a fishnet
my coconut body
sways toward you
watch the sun burst forth!

The Hawaiian Sugarcane
Wild Boar Manong

Listening to manong lomanta
will drive you crazy
Everything he says is upside-down
When I say up he says down
When I say down he says up
All his learning comes
from chasing wild boar
in the sugarcane fields
Women come knocking
on his door at all hours
Nothing can keep them away
Money comes on the first
and third of every month
Everything is gone in a few days
Silk-laced panties hang
from his door
The glare in his eyes
can swallow you up
Life goes on no matter what
Throwing his head back
Twisting his lips

The Wandering Manong

I am not ashamed of the manong, nor do I feel
sad by their tragic story in America. The manongs
have been on a long journey and I have been one
of those wanderers who they have met along the
way. What right does anyone have to judge these
manongs who have come to America seeking for a
new life. They have lived through so many wars
and have scars in their hearts to prove it. They
were the brown gypsies, the low-down niggers, the
brown apache savages, the uncivilized nomads who
wandered from place to place in search of their
dreams. They left the waterbuffalo at home. Even
the waterbuffalo was led home with an iron ring
strung around its nose. The manongs threw the
ring across the ocean. They lived, as it were, in
two worlds—in a world they left behind, and in a
dream before their eyes.

the manong's voice
changes from day to day
winter snowfall
sun & moon & stars
a wild spirit gone crazy
from mountain to mountain
from river to river
from tree to tree
from stream to stream
from fish to fish
from waterbuffalo to waterbuffalo
from bolo to bolo
from mango to mango
from coconut to coconut

from ifugao to t'boli
from forest to forest
from herding sheep to herding sheep
from herding cows to herding cows
from fruit picker to fruit picker
from alaska to alaska
from manilatown to manilatown
inside a pocket
a handful of fish
in the other
some rice
what else?
chewing shreds of
dried squid
heading toward the glowing sunset
in front a waterbuffalo
in back a waterbuffalo
on both sides a waterbuffalo
nothing else!
only what's up ahead
i asked a waterbuffalo what's up
watching it gather up shreds of
manilatown dreams
where are all the manongs?
"they're dead and gone, none of them left"
here and there are traces of fish
fish in brown hands hang on
i made it to manilatown
the people here can name every fish back home
they sang songs all night
waiting so long for the international hotel
i dreamt of a place to gather with them
surrounded with trees and rivers
who could have caused the manongs such pain?
i remember the rains running down their faces
writing down all their stories

in spring, summer, autumn, & winter
drinking wine with manong espiritu & asoria
talking to the winter rain
oh, how they can laugh
oh, how they can laugh
they never had time for books
yet they can read the winter rains
what is this place they call home
why write anything down
hold on to the waterbuffalo's tail
before it slips away.

Taxi Dance

taxi dance
8 p.m.–2 a.m.
blondies
seven days a week

"i forgot
my labors
for awhile
at the taxi dance"

the hand around
your waist
feels good

is nothing
but my own

belonging to nobody
but to you
if you want it

"they're all blondies
most of the women
all mataba from the south"

but the goddamn tickets
for you
went so fast

into three minutes
ten-cent squeezes

"ten cents a dance
for three minutes
maybe the pinoy loses all money

i lost five dollars in one night
i think the girls get paid two dollars
a night, there was some trouble
in the taxi dances, the pinoy fight
over the woman, they get jealous.
after dancing you can accompany them
to eat, but those so-called gang
leaders are waiting for the girls
outside, and if they don't like
your face, they will fight with you."

my hands
know better

the fat juicy grapes
left behind

in the florin orchards
fit so nicely between my fingers

my hands
know better

the grapes

than
the lining of your body.

Manong O'Campo

crosses the tenderloin street
dressed in old, clean goodwill
sunday best
straight up to this manong
meeting o'campo 15 years later
lit up the city streets
1920 s.f. bound
honolulu taxi-dance halls
swinging to "my heart is sad
& lonely
for you i cry. . . for you dear only"
filling up his old tired eyes
"no big thing. why it's only ten
cents a dance."

wild memories spring up
sparkle like crystal snow flakes
spitting out kearny street
bakero tales
records i-hotel uprising spirits
on the tip of his tongue
stained with bagoong
tangled in balikbayan dreams
searching for the other half
of the waterbuffalo

"it'll be good if i last one year
good enough!
i'm 90 years old. . . ready to die!"

manong o'campo's eyes push far back

old tired bones ache
brittle as summer leaves.

Bataan Bar in Delano

kid danny
twenty years
is a long time
to be away
from home
your brown fist
put money
in your pocket
you kept winning
every fight
if you go home to hawaii
your heart will be
in the right place
now you're sitting
in the bataan bar
in delano
drinking beer
thinking
about the past
your white girlfriend
carries your portfolio
of your life
but you can walk
without your portfolio
you got eighty fights
young brown brother
the streets will always
smell of wine
picking grapes
for $3.68 an hour
isn't worth it
you can't even afford rice
or the young whores

who push on you
if the grapes
take time
to ripen
why shouldn't the
manong
take a whole season
to make love

Jurimentado Blues in Reno

manong samposa

was it worth
the anger

in a bolo

to get the jurimentado blues

in reno

was it worth
the anger

in a bolo

to grab a white man

by the neck

because

he laughed at you

did it feel good

manong

to jerk him hard
three times

until

you nearly broke his neck

was it better
to go crazy

and get the jurimentado blues

leaving three marks

around his neck

or to lose two hundred dollars

in blackjack

Photo by Chris Huie

Lucky M Poolhall, San Francisco

Guadalupe:
"Come To Me My Melancholy Baby"
(for norman jayo)

Tino's barbershop
Manila Cafe: adobo rising from carabao plates
Lucky "M" poolhall
Pin stripe, gabardine, english tweed, worsted
Macintosh double-breasted, single-breasted, cara-
Breasted, pinoy-breasted suits
50-60 years of dreams and nightmares
Rising out of mudfish eyes
Shrimp dances hidden in the Louisiana swamps
Brown feet stomping to Bogobo beats
Pinoys left hugging coconut trees
Damp with leftover semen
Brown flesh clinging to Louisiana blondies
Stretched across the velvet cloth pooltables
Her long legs crossed over like a manilatown crucifix
Apoy, apoy between the legs
Showing only part of her lily-white legs
(How slender her legs while brown hands slowly move up
And down—searching for the opening. . .
oh a sampagita flower!)
Hidden somewhere in the Cagayan jungles
Hands slowly move up—making the sigh of the cross
Genuflecting to the blondie—the goddess of lucky "M"
The green bills stick like biko
Titillating erections: fives, tens, twenties, fifties
The pinoys reach for a golden kiss
Brown, fat, thick lips purple as clouds over Mindanao
Imperial valley heat rises in the body
Flamed like a raging bull after the sun
Louie Syquia slides the bills inside the blondie's blouse
Take 5. Shoot 5. Don't shoot. I shoot already. I mean

I shot. Goddamn it—don't shoot. I mean shoot. Shooting
Again. Get the hands in there. Inside. No! Inside here.
In her blouse like you mean it, Louie. That's it. O.K.
One more time. Like you really mean it. That's it. Yeah!
What a take! I mean what a shot. I shoot already. You shot.
Goddamn it...oh shit! This is a take. Hold it now. All right!
Your titi! Re-shoot. I love it is the same as I lobe it.
Cut. Don't cut. Shoot. Oh shit! I shot. Go ahead and shoot!
Shoot! Oh shit. I shot. Oh, what a shot! I mean what a cut.
Shut your mouth. Wait! "Come to me my melancholy baby."
Oh god! Shoot inside her blouse. O.K. Let's shoot again.
Oh shit!
"Louie—this time really mean it." Cut. He shot.
Oh beautiful!

Carlos Bulosan: Pilipino Poet

carlos bulosan
pilipino poet

the manongs held you
down to the old cot

unbuckled
your leather belt

that kept
your thin t.b. body

together

yanked off your pantaloon
and then retreated

in the background
of music and playing cards

left your naked body
lying there alone

trembling with a woman

you kept
the cries down

for only a moment

wiping the pain away
releasing the milky sap

in pure savage-brown ecstasy

but lasting no more
that a split second

the first and last embrace
of a naked pilipino man
and a chicana woman

brown arms clinging
around each other

breathing

hot summer sweat

but it ended

because
it held nothing

but a zero
in a pocket
of erections

like a sweet dream
inside a warm opening

gone away

remembering nothing
but the words

of the woman

"do you like it?"
"do you like it?"

II
Back
To
The
Land

Back to the Land

ninety-six miles   Hawaii
a straight, twisting
narrow stretch
old hawaiian weather-beaten
rusty tin-roof shacks
spread along two sides
of the road
green coconuts & banana palms
sway against the sky
the water sparkles
heading over to jim's & tais's land
nobody in his right mind would travel here
who knows the real meaning of this land
nothing's here but molten lava rocks
jagged & sharp like knives
Cutting under your brown feet
only a mind that knows what is far
and near can tread on this land
the land never ends
found this place a long time ago
when the rains and rivers pulled them thru
a hundred thousand dreams
They know the lava rocks come
from mother earth
grass and weeds can grow on this land
flowers grow wild
pulling up a bunch of weeds
yellow & green
jim says "right here!"
digging in deep
replanting some cactus
"it'll take!" "it'll take"
"it'll survive!"

lay down rocks
protecting the land
coming back here
next year
fifty feet away
planting europoia —— root "Europe"
(a horn-like african plant)
pele knows the ancient spirit
she's no stupid goddess
"get the small, skinny, tall one
put it over by the ohia lava tree."

bring it all together
and make it
native

Hidden Forest Sanctuary

"An old man owns the house behind that tree."
Passed two weather-beaten shacks before we go
any further. After a short, heavy rain—we head up
a narrow path. Thick mud covers the silent path.
Thirty or fifty acres stretch in the mists.
Thousands of trees rise above the hills. Dark green fern
scattered down below. My brother leads uphill
thru and thru endlessly—follow his brown forest
spirit. "I'll build a bridge right here." Up a steep hill.
"I'll build a house right here." The silence is deep.
"And a tea house right over there." We need only
to open up—to free ourselves and let all nature
enter and flow until we have become immersed
completely. We have to immolate ourselves—to give
our spirits up to the flow until we have become
one with the rock, mountains and hills. . . like we are
ascending Mt. Omine, celebrating our inner spirit—
a silent journey, an eternal retreat; we touch the
Ogamiysan Ascetic healers. We need to summon
the mountain spirits—draw them within us. . .
to beat the center of our hara, feeling the skin on
our face—like feeling the universe for the first time.

Ano no ue
Ten shojo chi shojo
Ten shojo chi shojo
Naige shojo rokkon shojo
Yoribito wa
Ima zo yorikuru
Nagahama no
Ashige no koma ni
Tazuna yurikake

"Pure in heaven and pure in earth
Pure within and pure without
Pure in all six roots. . . you who
loosen now the reins of your gray
horse as you gallop to me over the
long beach."

High above the hills. . . my mind slowly
soaks in—feeling the tall thin weeds
bending inside of me. The grass covers
my body and my eyes swallow the deep
silence. Birds in the distance—not
one sound. My brother's name moves thru
the forest like a wild animal—each
step of the way he knows by heart.
Every branch is a rib in his chest.
Every tree is filled with his spirit.
Every hill in the forest sings his
silent songs. Each drop of rain is his
life. He's more at home naked and more
naked at home. He moves in rain, mists,
and fog. Even insects circle round his
feet. Name says, "Deer in the forest
urinate apple blossoms. Temple abbots
wipe their asses clean with bark and
then run naked into the moon."
My brother treads uphill on the "edge
of life and death." He whips around
like a deer zigzagging. "Right here will
be a bridge." I follow him thru mist,
fog and rain. Footsteps as sacred as
the forest's gods. He knows more of nature
because he travels its forbidden paths—
and because all of his learning comes
directly from trees, rocks, mountains,
bones, and fish in the ocean, river and

streams. All he has learned comes from
nothing. Why just the other day he read a
poem in the fish scales of a silver salmon,
scattered them in the air. He removed the
fish bones and rattled them and danced to
the black bears in the sky. Snow cranes
high above the hills. Rain beats down.
Treading over the grass—my spirit rises
to meet my brother in the heavy downpour,
heading toward the northern hill.
Name—wild spirit of the rain forest.
For seventeen years he poured and drank tea
in my teahouse—and for seventeen years
his spirit grew. And now we meet each other
again, after many years—we meet under dark
clouds, treading thru the rainforest; together we
head for the highest mountain in the rain.

Jedediah Smith Redwoods

(for Mee Har)

a walking-stick mind
holding up two hundred pounds
wobbling down the path
limping to wind branches
rubbing sounds
camping under giant redwoods
cushioned on a blanket of
fallen leaves & branches

del norte is up ahead
what one needs. . . is a little
or nothing

carrying cooked rice to the
jedediah smith redwoods
bringing along green tea—
sipping tea. . . mornings
afternoons & evenings

talk with moon, the head chief
ask him how are the relatives
doing up there
played with the sky-children

laying down my mind on
mountains & redwoods
meditate on nothing
wind-sweeping
north south
east west

*Native American
imagery*

left everything behind
a few lines of poetry
bird scratchings—
bear tracks
in rivers
my spirit crosses
spreads far and wide
as a bald mountain
wind-spread eagle

Traveled North to the Woods
Humboldt to Oregon–Washington
Pacific Northwest Cascades

sharp jagged peaks
stretch high
push up to the sky
mountains rise strong
and tall in the morning
bend and sleep all night
long
rocky green hills
twist and turn
disappear in the fog
no wandering chinese hermits
wind-stomping around here
no wild tongue flapping taoist sages
shooting fire out of their fingers
tread in these winter snow parts
no sign of raging buddhist nuns
urinating plum blossoms in the cold stream
not even tao chie'n is here
laughing up the dead spirits
dangling his dirty feet
in a wooden tub of cow dung wine
black-brown mountains
spread far south
roads whip around narrow cliffs
snow on mountain tops
slowly breaks up
stop to watch
the water flow
down the mountainside
into skagit river

Hwy 101
sees only whites

skagit river
fresh winter cold

where are the indians?
dead in the ground?
no blacks seen around here
licking white cotton
no chicanos or pilipinos
in the valleys or fields
not even one chinaman drying
seaweed or catching fish
not even one japanese farmer
seen turning the soil

Boyang the Wandering Recluse

Boyang–Boyang–Boyang–Boyang–Boyang
The northern wind sweeps the mind clear
into a thousand dreams, drawing Boyang
farther & farther & deeper & deeper
into the "snows of life"—your bamboo
flute cuts across, echoes, and cuts
thru the thick icebergs—vibrating layers
of the mind that circle the Bering Sea.
Loneliness grabs the heart, filling it with
burning portraits of "women of the past."
How many women have given their lives up
for you?. . . their minds sweetened your taste
buds—their pale bodies clung to your
wandering bamboo flute.

Boyang–Boyang–Boyang–Boyang–Boyang
How deep is the silence of winter?
How far is the journey?
When the paths covered in snow
No longer welcome the ancient songs
Your long bamboo flute brings back snow-memories
Has the snow fallen?
Mountains grow tall and sad
Flowers waiting to bloom
Frozen silence
Still-dreams
Boyang–Boyang–Boyang–Boyang–Boyang
The snow is still thick around
Your bamboo flute.

Kenji Miyazawa, the Sad Poet

I feel very close to Kenji Miyazawa, the sad poet
of Japan. . . somehow he draws me closer to nature.
He was born in Iwate, in the northern part known
as the "Tibet of Japan." He was a Buddhist and
steeped in a reservoir of disciplines—the Lotus
Sutra was his life. He believed in the so-called
six realms of existence into which enlightened
beings are repeatedly born.

He says, "You say you suffer
if you do suffer. . .
you better go walk in the rain
and stay in the woods of bamboo and oak
(Get your hair cut. . . because you've got
hair like that
you think things like that)."

My hair is long
No need to cut it
even in the rain
moss will grow
knots on it.
once again
I am driven toward
the water
the northern mountains
grab my mind
I speak with rivers
flowing from high
mountain ranges
the mountain snow forest
freezes my mind still.

Photo by Louis Brian Smith

Al Robles and Sakurai Takamine, 1960

Sakurai Takamine, the Wandering Kyushu Mountain-Sake Hobo

one flower blooms
a black bird sings
sakurai treads north
a deer zigzagging across

sakurai: "nothing but loneliness
a thousand kyushu eyes
a universe of flowers
pounding mochi in the new year's rain
brings a river of sad tears
worn wooden getas tilts back the mind
manyōshu mountain songs
echo fukuoka dreams
ancient tales flow from bancha
sushi all night long
midnight bush street kyushu mt. sake
nightmares rise out of ragged kimono sleeves
rice, sardines and wine
winter koicha tatami-silence
cha-no-yu all year round
sip usucha
kyushu forest. . . sound of getas
mountain snow packed inside old robes
tread around snowcapped mountain
songs of children cry out: ara-san–ara-san–ara-san
your childhood songs inside your heart:
ame, ame, ame, ame. . . come on!

pass sake after sake around a mountaintop
thundering noh sounds echo from afar
taiko drums rain sushi-songs

sit on a wood floor inside a circle
waterbuffaloes dance to kyūgen ghosts
rice harvest songs
drunk all night with kyushu mt. sake:
a long drunken kyushu mountain-sake hobo journey—
wading into a river of salmon. . . .

o art is my life. . . o life is my art
eyes are like a mouth. . . they talk too much
sadness is over my life."

oh, nichiren buddha women!
don't bow too low. . . sakurai
will stick you from behind—
thunderbolt!

oh, run buddha women!
run thru sakurai's open door
no thick wooden buddha temple gates
to keep you inside
tumble over konnyaku's tail

chanting brings no enlightenment
strip-down naked—kyoto pubic-moss
sip koicha
between heaven and earth
the flushing wind sound of konnyaku's tail
opens the mind into winter snow
gong and bells suffocate the heart
make koicha with gasoline and ashes
set it to blaze in the rain
soto zen monks smoke dope
slapped a rinzai monk on the back
"fuck you! fuck you!. . . motherfucker!"

puff on a cloud
the full moon
drink snow water
dump buddha's robe
down konnyaku's toilet

drown in kyushu mountain-sake
caught the wandering spirit
in nanao's eyes: thin cheekbones
tall and skinny
like kyoto weeds—
sitting quietly.

sakurai-san: "i want your shi-poetry
i want your life. . ."

one cup of sake
raw tuna
morning mist
sound of footsteps
oh, a naked woman!

rain all night
feet soaked—mind drained
heart full of rainwater. . . what else?
what next? nothing but a full moon:
a kinoki branch sways.

konnyaku: a hobo zen cat that chases after raw fish
a mind zigzags around bamboo and rocks
leaving no tracks—washes down in the rain
no trace of semen
swallows down sharp winter bamboo leaves
coughing up thunder-river sounds.

insects and parasites in his thick hide
turns them loose inside a bush street teahouse
what's more? left muddy imprints of his ugly face
on the kitchen walls.
(konnyaku's balls hang loose like sakurai's mind)

insects, parasites. . .
even in winter
scratching wind-songs
run, run konnyaku
here comes musashi
the crazy rinzai zen monk
with a long penis
in his hand—

let the insects and parasites
run off with the sexual disease
oh, konnyaku leave your dung
on the tatami mats
temple bells don't ring out anymore
spread your fur in the kyushu mountain wind
sakurai's rock feet smashes bush street
cockroaches in the dark
life between zen toes is worth nothing

"the moon is like my eyes, they see too much"
(it's me!. . . sakurai-san!. . . it's me!)
"he's a tea master, you know. . . like child
i like his tea, you know—simple."
konnyaku's songs underneath brown feet
cling to sakurai's mind like seaweed on rocks.

Ryōkan–The Crazy Snow Poet

Reading this poet makes me wonder who's crazy?
They say he was born in 1758 in the village of
Izumozaki in Echigo province now called Niigata
on the north-west coast of Japan. They called him
Eizo when he was a child. There are times when
I feel like Ryōkan running free and crazy in the snow.
I didn't know until later on how crazy I was
stripping down naked. . . running wild thru big
bear snow country. I dug a hole and laid down
my mind. Remembering how Ryōkan lived in his shack. . .
his whole mind covered in snow and nothing else.
He drank tea around the clock. A few years back
I carried rocks from the Tuolumne river and
gathered wood all year round for a teahouse. That's
crazy! Ryōkan was a simple poet who believed in
mountain snow-silence and the freedom to be himself.
Nothing else really matters.

A Mountain-Toilet Thief

A mountain-toilet thief
ran off with Mee Har's breasts

Mee Har carries a mountain
of sadness
in each breast
and it sagged

and the birds wailed, wailed, wailed
loud

Winter-Buddha face
yellow autumn-skin
Empty mountain-breasts
lips wet as early spring
and tight as two ripe persimmons

I am a wild mountain-toilet thief
ran off with Mee Har's
young mountain-breasts

Four seasons—turned the soil
Scattered a thousand saplings
Fog covered the past
Left a young mountain-breast
with the emptiness
of Buddha
Wiped Buddha clean with toilet paper
and threw it to the wind.

Hunting for Bamboo

Bamboo fills my mind
swimming up mountains
the fish bring back songs
following jim & tais
looking for green bamboo
all four laid-out
on the roadside
wild bamboo dreams stretch
toward the mountains
(my brother knows the secrets
of bamboo)
scattering leaves
wild geese
remembering
in winter
how he cut the
coconuts
one by one
handing them to me
falling
from the sky
gathering fish
& raw octopus

pele, the goddess
cannot sit down with
some stupid haole
and tell them to leave
the lava rocks alone
my brother knows better
broke out with giant sores
all over his legs
threw the rocks back to

pele, the goddess of
the volcano
the sores peeled off
like ripe bananas
in the boiling sun
learning how to turn back
my mind to natural things
tracing all those footsteps
in the bamboo forest
hear songs loud and clear
from raw fish to cooked rice

Sushi-Okashi and Green Tea
with Mitsu Yashima

cherry blossom spring festival
outside yashima's window
a cedar sways
looking northeast
remnants of konnyaku's past
a buried teahouse
under a slab of cement
splintered bamboo memories
rise up in the fog
nihonmachi tambourines
turn into kokeshi dolls
hidden behind moth-eaten shintō robes
michiko's koto strings break the silence
taiko drums
pound mochi
into snow
mitsu yashima
born in kobe
california—1950
seventy-five-year-old issei woman—
oh ageless child!
swim the river
in the sky
"i want to be free from everything—
from everybody"

i hear
your brush strokes
in the wind
painting a river
in the sky

drinking the tea
sushi and manju
we need not ask for more
only our teacups
remained empty
yashima-san
your laughter moves
a thousand hokkaido mountains
i'll carry a thousand-pound sushi
for you—and scatter manju to flying cranes
in the spring rain

Meeting the Poet Luis Syquia
On the Fourth Month
Thirteenth Day One Thousand
Nine-Hundred-Eighty-Nine

We meet again at another time and place
Up on a hill & far away from manilatown
From tribal memories of the international
Hotel. Away from sounds of the manongs
Away from ifugao myths and dreams.
We meet like two crazy wandering poets
In the midst of guitar music.
We meet for the first time only because
We left behind our minds, soaked inside
A giant porcelain vat of fermented shrimps
Salmon eggs, pig entrails, eagle feathers
Balot, water-buffalo tails and monkey skulls.
We meet like two salmon returning upriver
Returning home, carrying nothing but the
Sound of water . . . tubig. Wind slapping
Each other on the back. Smashing everything
In the past. What's left rattles like memories
Two poets meeting over grass and rocks—rising
To a new spring moon. And all we have left over
Is a mountain belly full of laughter. Like two
Ragged manongs, in agbayani winter village rags
Falling over each other in the california grape
Orchards . . . . drunk with the coconut feelings of
Brown people. Rice foaming in the mouth—
Everything from ifugao myths to t'boli tales
And dreams. How else can two poets meet?

Mary Tall Mountain

from a village far north in alaska
a village of a hundred indians
a snow country of wolves and bears
a village bound by mountains
hills, rivers, streams and trees
a koyukon athabascan
born in nulato, alaska
the sound of the yukon river
tells you where to go
two rivers: koyukuku and yukon
meet together and become one
who knows the wilderness
best? only a mind that knows
the way home. only a snowbound
spirit knows the path back.
find mary tall mountain's place
in the wilderness of my mind
stirring dreams sparkle
branches twist and bend in the mind
a heap of bear droppings froze
far and wide
the animals begin to lead back home
up over hills willows bend
fox, lynx, bear, marten, wolverine,
mink, beaver, muskrat, otter,
moose and deer
what does mary tall mountain
know of the wilderness?
everything free runs wild
in the mind
where does she find her place
in the wilderness?
when the two rivers: koyukuku

and yukon pass her place
when the snow falls
a mind soaks in deep
mary tall mountain lives alone
in the tenderloin
books on four walls
stacked to the ceiling
shows me an unfinished novel
in three stages
talking about writing, poetry, poets
and life
listening to her laughter
shakes the four corners
of the world

i rise up like a black bear
meeting the mountains, rocks,
trees, rivers, streams, skies,
hills, weeds, grasses. . .
meeting the sun
upon my face
hunting for blackberries
leaving a long trail of mountain bear
blackberry droppings
(rubus ursinus)
unloading my mind

mountain forest grass
lead me on
stepping over rocks
over a natural lesson
of rivers, suns, moons, stars
snows, redwoods

where otter
quail, bluejay

scribble songs on
smith river-rocks
a salmon
wheel of life
birth rebirth

a graveyard with no gravestones
rattling bones in deep silence

bears and deer
lapping up water

rivers, creeks, streams

wrapping up a mind in deerskin
strapping down ryōkan's
snow poems

traveling with a wild mind
pushing back city life
and dreams
a bear mind
running wild
in my mind.

Wandering North to Alaska

traveling back and forth
to the old world
animal bones haunt his wild spirit
he can see the markings of ice and snow
walruses swim in and out of holes
sledding clear across two worlds
he can follow the moon when rivers
freeze up and when they flow again
he haunts for old songs in the coldest days
polar bears keep wandering up and down
he waits for the ungrook under the ice
jayo sings snow songs
to those who will listen
in late spring nothing moves
everything stands still
only a few boats between shore and pack ice
willows grow in the river valleys
in summer flowers bloom
rose, anemone, mosses, sedges, mustard
grasses and lichen
breathing in the while season
crossing over the tundra
into a world of emptiness
learning from the inupiat
left behind the moose, caribou and salmon
wolverines, wolves and deer
just finished eating whale meat
a dark brown pinay asked jayo,
"do you speak inupiat?"
he heaved up snow and growled.
muktuk-muktuk-muktuk-muktuk
muktuk-muktuk-muktuk-muktuk

Winter Rain Yum Cha with Gin San

Winter rain yum cha with Gin San
A fat, sloppy, ragged, dirty, nose-
picking recluse, who hangs out at
Portsmouth Square all year-round.

Dragonflies get all tangled up in
his thick black mountain hair
Knotted with pine cones
White insects big as rice grains
crawl in and out.

Gin San's body smells of coconut
wine and rotten fish heads
Rats curl up at his feet
Nothing can keep them away.

Three hundred pounds of tough, hard
mongolian hide drags on the wet grass
His belly sags like rain-soaked clouds
Loose like fish tails in the wind.

Gin San lays back after a pot of tea
Pulls open his shirt and laughs
Black hairy mushrooms sprout out
Drunken buddhas cling to his wind-blown
mountain-weathered hands.

Cheuk Heuk Returns to Hong Kong One More Time

flying over to hong kong
to a buddhist funeral
shopping for two colors
white on white
black on black
who would know the difference?
bowing to the dead in white
will not raise up the dead
bowing to the dead in black
will not raise up the dead
sitting in silence with families
from america
burning incense will not rub away the pain
the body of cheuk heuk's uncle waits
to be cut open like a winter melon
no death certificate
no documents come forth
the body sits in ice
waiting for words to be heard
tangled in rice paper
the earth cries out once more
opening itself to cushion another body
the ancient ghosts rise up everywhere
hovering over the earth like dark clouds
ten thousand spirits throw up
unfulfilled dreams
desires run wild
rambling on and on
grabbing on to "one hundred things of the past"
minds twist up and down
apples and oranges pile up high
on the altar of the dead

cheuk heuk knows the place of her own mind
tears rise like a wild river
no kind of buddhist ceremony will help matters
the pain passes thru trees like the wind
cheuk heuk–cheuk heuk–cheuk heuk
a sweet river flows out of your mouth

Over Etang's House For Talong

eggplant

Salmon and onions and tomatoes
and a soup with upo-like squash
etang–etang–etang–etang–etang

Back home in Sorsogon
The fish smells strong
Nothing smells like it
Anywhere in the world
Someone asked, "How do you
Cook fishhead soup?"
Etang answered, "First,
Catch a fish with a big head
Be sure its eyes are clear and
A river flows thru it
When that is all done
Swim in its belly."

Wahat Tampao said, "No one
Makes sense anymore."
Why all this fuss about
Cooking fishhead soup?
When you have fish you
Cook it, either with
Vegetables or over a fire
Last night some friends had
Fish with rice. Fish over
Rice is simple. In the village
That's all we eat.
Life goes on like that every day.
What does Etang mean by rivers
In the eye of the fish
The fish-eyes reflect the sky,
River, moon and stars.

A hundred things are mirrored
In its eyes. When we see the
World as the fish sees it, then
We can be free from attachments.

The fish possesses nothing
Yet it depends on the water
For its life.
But Etang says a river passes thru
the eyes of the fish.

Hop Jok Fair

Mee Har
The crazy moon woman
Ate a full plate
Of chow mein
Two pieces of lumpia
One slice of watermelon
Then swallowed down
Two cups of oolong tea
Spinning the day
Round Portsmouth Square
Pounding two chinese drums
Winning two pounds of rice

Hop Jok Fair Portsmouth Square
Watched Mee Har
The crazy moon woman
And Konnyaku
The Nihonmachi alley cat
Leap high above
Portsmouth Square Bridge
With a hundred children
Chasing after a red dragon
Grabbing hold of
The dragon's tail
Whipping it round
Spreading the sky yellow

Shan Mei
Longtime friend
Many years back
Pale-autumn face
Snowbound mind

Dark eyes
Strong and clear
Reaches out on the grass
Pushing up the past

Hop Jok Fair Portsmouth Square
Manong Amoite
73-year-old
Farm worker
Sitting up straight
On a wooden bench
Like young asparagus
In the Salinas fields
Touching Ilocano hands

One black man
Tattered clothes
Like shredded grass
Says to me,
"Say, brother—
give me some watermelon."
Two big juicy
Red slices
Cut just right
Put between
Two big black hands
With only a few bites
And it goes down so easy

Hop Jok Fair Portsmouth Square
Brought the people together
All the young and old
Swallowing the sun

A NEW DAY RISING
SHOOTING UP
LIKE FRESH PAMPAS GRASS

Holiday Inn
Stand tall and dead
Yet down below
The flowing stream
Is alive
Loud and clear.

Poor Man's Bridge/Portsmouth Square

Poor man's bridge
Portsmouth Square
Forty pine trees scattered
Trimmed and pruned
Two trees dug out
A few flowers bloom

The pine branches
Cut in and out
Green and brown pine needles
A few horseflies on top

Persimmon-moon
Three yellow faces
Two children
On a swing
Swing back and forth
In the wind
Yellow-blue
Thru the trees
Round round faces
Fresh as a thousand autumns

Poor man's bridge
Portsmouth Square
Pulls down dark shadows
Old men and women sleep
Spring away

No more children's playground
Empty sandbox

Swings lay dead in the wind
Tangled across

The cold icy bars
No legs dangling thru

Poor man's bridge
Portsmouth Square
Yesterday
Only yesterday
The children's faces
Twirled thru the wind
Their tiny bodies played
Hopscotch with passing clouds

Poor man's bridge
Portsmouth Square
The sun is buried underneath
The cold cement

Far gone is the laughter
That grows tall in Spring
Far gone are the old Chinese women
With ancient cracked-white
Porcelain faces
Chattering in the long day sun
Far gone is spring

Poor man's bridge
Portsmouth Square
Six steel girder-branches
Blossoms half-a-block long
Stretching nowhere

Poor man's bridge
Portsmouth Square
Heavier than ten thousand
dung mountains

Dead spring.

III
Chinatown
Blues
For
Blues
Poets

Chinatown Blues for Blues Poets

chinatowns of america—run from coast to coast, from trinity
county to sisikyu mountains, from locke california, to king
street seattle, from stockton to San Francisco hidden cobble-
stone alleyways, from canton to fairfield. leongs, lims, chins, *writers*
wongs, laus, lees, choys, toms fill the chinatown landscape. *and*
gung yan rise like winter storms. steel rails whip around gold *poets*
mountain. blood & sweat flow deep two centuries back—
yangtze valley memories linger deep. back breaking gung
yan in tule swamps of the sacramento–san joaquin delta.
long black braids in the sierra wind—like whips whipping
the white snow where chinamen lay buried. screams from
chinatown dragons burn. gung yan fly from china camps, fly
home California chinatown, leaping with fire & shark fins.
canton vision in the eyes of george leong.

history of Chinese Immigration

Jazz of My Youth

i remember jazz of my youth
in the streets of fillmore
crossing over to cousin jimbo's bop city
where the green between his dark ebony fingers
flapped in the cool post street wind
take the A train & slide all the way down
listening to sounds close to the ground
fillmore street bound
jazz comin' 'round
conga tight skins crack
snapping
all day & all morn'
all night session
how high the moon
laying down in the back room
horns blowing to stars fell on alabama
as the night fog squeezed in
wailing sounds echoed in the air
the streets sparkled like stars
all the things you are
jazz of my youth
cruising over to soulsville
stepping over cords
guitar strings cutting loose on tenderly
jazz of my youth
jacks on sutter
jackson's nook
step back & be cool
head to the back room
thick smoke curling round
a brown pilipino man
blowin' it's almost like falling in love
hunched over a piano

a gray sharkskin overcoat
dark shades
brown fingers runnin' up & down
the ivory keys
dark black hair gleams
with three flowers
charlie abing
the jazz man from stockton
blowing sax & piano
what a rare mood i'm in
it's almost like falling in love
jazz of my youth
runnin' the mo
the cool streets
talkin' deep & sweet
i remember you. . . you're the one that
made my dreams come true. . .

Fillmore Black Ghetto

fillmore black ghetto
jackson's nook
dark shades
ghetto loneliness

three black cats
splitting sounds
breaking horns
"everything i have is yours"

cleanhead smith
wailing
funky blues
jack's
on sutter street

cousin jimbo's bop city
after hours
flip nuñez
cool brown fingers
blowing
"how high the moon"

ghetto riff
tight skins
ramie
blowing
"stars fell on alabama"

malis
"take the a train"
jamming
all the way

no time to stop
bebop express

armando rendon's
brown magic
finger tips
flaming
the congo soul

fillmore black ghetto
abraham lincoln
fucked on
japanese sake
ginza
red lights
runnin' after
young geishas
yoshiwara nightmares
ridin'
the toraya winds
chasin' after
lady murasaki shikibu
in the "tale of the genji" dreams

shirasagi bar
musashi's five-inch getas
kyoto sounds
ancient-drunk
sake-nights
empty zen jive
stoned buddha-heads
swallowing
rinzai-zeros
smashing

t'ang dynasty koans
with sapporo beer bottles

two-bit
southern white
witch doctors
jivin'
black magic
cheap-ass
love potion
rattling bones
35 cents
voodoo dolls
5 & 10 cents
needles

fillmore black ghetto
dirty dozen
mustard green sky
afro-red moon
sweet potato pie
hickory pit
charcoal-red hot links
barbecue spareribs
seven days a week

hamilton
crystal pool
rusti's
young bloods
floating high

lee's
black-japanese
tearoom
stoned cockroaches

sitting around cross-legged
on lacquered
goza mats

wooden getas
slidin' by
bush street
chop suey palace
sakurai's
99 cents

junk special
heavy spread
two ghetto pork chops
mashed potatoes
string beans
apple sauce
white bread
dessert & coffee

chinese meat market
tinted meat
stacked shit—high
salt pork blues
45 cents a pound

primalon ballroom
shufflin' time
round trip excursion
rampley's
24 hours
jango basement blues

red's
thick
slick

processed
cordovan brown
shoe shine
parlor
50 cents a shine

eddy street
dark safari hunt
pacific heights
limousines
cruisin'
up and down
honking down
young whores

fillmore station
blue moon cafe
blood
"i saw you standing alone
without a dream in your eyes"

molotov cocktail summer
cool jaimo
bustin'
night into day
like lightning
runnin' the Mo
leadin'
a hundred black dragons
with a steel fist

gray chicks
stoned high
tellin' lies
to cousin jimbo
gettin' down

playin' games
with twenty-dollar tricks

fillmore black ghetto
number 22 line
texas stomp
konked express

flyin' high
cocaine jive
weed pie

cozy corner
preacher john
laying down
the gospel
"get down on your knees
for jesus, you black sinners"

next stop
mcallister
soul food cookin'
grits
chittlin hog intestines
stuffed with sausages
ham hocks
beans and rice

muslim center
ellis & webster
brother nathaniel
rapping heavy
"whatcha name?
you ain't got no name
the white man gave you

your name.
the white man

was crawlin' around on his
hands and knees, yeah, brother
while the black man was walkin'
around upright

louisiana fish market
dark meat
big bone
louisiana
buffalo fish

melrose junction
hampton hawes
got it down
no other sound
"all the things you are"

misty
erroll garner
runnin'
up and down
the keyboard
black over white
"i only have eyes for you"
nothin' else will do
when you feelin' blue

black prince
sellin'
jive hot dogs
pushin' time
makin' a dime

talkin' fine
usin' that jive line

nylon stockings
wrapped tight
round black heads
sharp blades
sharkskin rags
alligator shoes
cool bloods

midnight
kinky ghetto head
todavo's
glass eyes
swallowing
african orchids
in mojo dreams

fillmore long bar
shufflin' back
black memories
dinah washington
singing
"september in the rain"
o lady day
what you got to say
don't do me that way
don't do me wrong
baby, sing me your song
"i got you under my skin"

denny's
barrelhouse bar
boogie woogie
all night long

chapel hill
baptist church
sunday morning stylin'

mo street blues
baby, baby, baby
i feelin' so bad
wake up this mornin'
feelin' so sad
cryin' so bad

baby, baby, baby
i ain't got nothin' to eat
wake up this mornin'
feelin' so sad
cryin' so bad

cadillac slim
midnight pimp
stompin'
ten-dollar tricks
for gray chicks
at the blue mirror

brown hands
unfolding
black flesh
dyin' pimps
laid out cold
on piss streets

up on cathedral hill
seven million dollars
st. mary's cathedral
mama of raving whores

two young bloods
holdin' onto
the archbishop's cape
daddy of ghetto nightmares
anointed pimp
walkin' down
the main aisle

down below
fillmore black ghetto
jivin' whores
hustlers
drivin' pimps
hip & slick hog snout
hot-water
corn bread
blackeyed peas
ain't all there is

soulsville
baby
what it is
starvin'
black children
jingle jangle
thru dark alleys
young bloods
poor blacks
reachin' & crawlin'
screamin' & hollerin'
at the white lies & promises
of holy men & politicians

Rebirth of Wounded Knee

Once Black Elk, a reed-thin Holy man
of the Oglala Sioux Tribe
Roamed the Black Hills in South Dakota
And spilled wild winter snow-tales
"of another world."

One day Black Elk painted his face red
and charged the soldiers with
his sacred bow
Bullets passed right by him
like the wind.

Loves War and Iron Wasichu were around then
looking down from Pine Ridge—
The gunfire was loud and clear.

The shooting below Pine Ridge
carried thru the wind and echoed
A thousand winter battles in the rain
like wild spirits shooting across
The vast plains.

The Sacred burial ground lies south
of Pine Ridge
And stretched far east and west.

Where is the Wichsha Wakon
roaming around now?
Why is she not around Wounded Knee
breaking the spirits loose?

LISTEN TO THE CRIES OF WOUNDED KNEE
LISTEN TO THE CRIES OF WOUNDED KNEE

The heavy guns shattered
women and children

The Wakan-Tanka spirit is more
than just grass bending in
The mind of a Lakota.

A handful of buffalo dung
has more spirit
Than a hundred thousand white men.

" A THUNDER BEING NATION I AM, I HAVE SAID
A THUNDER BEING NATION I AM, I HAVE SAID
YOU SHALL LIVE
YOU SHALL LIVE
YOU SHALL LIVE
YOU SHALL LIVE"

Red blood Lakota faces
mount your wild horses
Charge with your sacred bows
drive the white man out
of your sacred ground.

Come rescue your people
grab their hands
Wrap their naked bodies with
a thousand summer buffalo hides.

One hundred winters ago
a Wakan woman
Appeared to two Lakota
hunting for game around Wounded Knee.

The Lakota's eyes ran wild
after the Wakan woman's body

The beauty of the Wakan woman
bends a thousand cedar trees
And is like a thunderbolt
inside a Lakota's mind. . .
Splitting open hidden mountain-red desires
and rising like one-hundred-foot waves
Pushing up like jagged mountains—
touching the heavens
And flaming like a hundred volcanoes.

The Wakan woman turned one Lakota
into a sandbag of winter bones
And the snakes swallowed him up—
even in the wind the bones did not rattle
The Wakan woman told the other pure flowing water
mind Lakota—with fresh grass-rain tongue
To carry the message to Hehlokecha Hajin.
The burning red warriors swallowed
the wakan-tanka spirit
and they were proud and strong
women sang a thousand songs
to the great spirit
then bundled their little ones
in buffalo skin
waited for their men
to return from battle
so the feast can begin.

After the long battle
a spring mouthful of buffalo meat—
then swallow the full moon.

The white man has sucked onto
the sioux indians' peace pipe
too long
too long

now the white buffalo cow woman has blossomed

flowering from
a steel gun barrel
remembering—

THE STONE COLD—1890 MASSACRE
OF WOUNDED KNEE

LISTEN TO THE CRIES OF WOUNDED KNEE
like a broken autumn kinoki branch
falling on the wet grass
red blood cries pulled
down blue skies
sioux-mohawk-navaho-hopi arrows
burnt the dark night pain
one hundred seasons of buffalo-silence
hidden underneath the white man's gun
sharp apache winds echoed
hunting memories buried deep
buckskins flapped
in a crying sacred grave
alcatraz tales pound
like a giant rock drum
the sound of a thousand whitetail deer.

The autumn battle alone is sad
Bitter cold winter
Frozen hands and feet of children
break in the snow.

Spring battles bring nothing
but hollow-splintered pain
And what good is summer
when the grasses are plentiful
And the buffalo is gone

A full stomach is worth more
Than dead grass.

Storm over Pine Ridge
across the creek to Wounded Knee
Lakotas–Lakotas–Lakotas–Lakotas–Lakotas
Lakotas–Lakotas–Lakotas–Lakotas–Lakotas

The spirit of Black Elk
grows strong in the warrior's heart
Let the northern geese circle round
Wounded Knee
and cool the spring pain.

The Wakan-Tanka spirit lives mountain strong
in trees, grass, mountains, rivers & streams—
Once this white buffalo cow woman
carried the Sacred pipe to the Sioux.

It is said that the white buffalo cow-woman
will appear again
At the end of this "world."

The Sacred pipe will bring back 300 dead
Sioux Indians
Massacred at Wounded Knee.

The Ghost Dance will not be empty of
crying winds
Whirling inside a blazing
Sioux's mind.

Laughing spirits will rise
and grow wild corn
And the buffalo will come to life.

It Was A Warm Summer Day

Listen to this:

It was a warm summer day
And I was out in the park
strolling without a worry
in the world.

And I came to a bench where
a middle-aged couple sat
feeding the birds & yapping
about Vietnam & Cambodia

They turned and looked at me
And said, "Are you Pilipino?"
And I said no.

Then they asked me
if I were Mexican.
And I said no.

Then they asked me
if I were Japanese
And I said no.

Then they asked me
if I were Chinese
And I said no.
And then they started to look at
each other & the birds kept
flapping their wings
And they looked at each other
& the birds kept flapping their wings
And said, "You must be Korean."

It was a warm summer day
And I was strolling in the park
without a worry in the world
And this couple had to ask me
questions like that.

I told them to keep feeding the
birds and quit asking me any more
stupid questions like that.
And they looked at each other
again and smiled and then said, "Son
we're on America's side. Come on tell
us! Where did you come from?"

I told them I clean toilets
And they got so angry at me
they called me all kinds of names.

And they still wanted to find out
who I was and where I came from.

They started to give me some crumbs
And they wanted me to open my mouth
& tell them everything.

I kept on telling them I was against
America. And they got so angry at me
& told me to go back where I came from
And I sat there lookin' at the trees
and the birds
And they just kept on yapping away
And they just kept on yapping away
louder & louder, "Why don't
you go back where you came from?"

I told them I jumped out of my mama's
womb & goddamn it if I could jump back
in there I do it right now
And they got so angry at me & threw
the crumbs right in my face and I laughed
so hard & I laughed so hard my belly ached.
And I knew I had to be on my way
'cause I had my belly full.

Olongapo

Helicopters hover overhead
while brown faces of
the young pinays stare
up at the US sailor boys
sailing off like a puff of
whipcream
wings of white angels
taking them by ships
waiting their departure
olongapo city
dances to the tune of
mayor gordon
the pimp of olongapo
young go-go dancers
strip down naked
to the brown
the color of the ground
prostrating on the stage
where white sailor boys
lick the sweat between
their legs
they have nothing else to show
only their white dicks
protruding out of their mouths
the virgin lays up all night
waiting to be laid by a sailor boy
with a stack of cheap-ass green
shriveling up like shit paper
the girls from the barrios
yearn for a white man to take them away
while their papa and mama wait at home
thinking their daughter is cleaning some church
while the virgin mary rises up in the cathedral
behind all the cigar smoke

hidden in the glowing ember of poverty
her arms stretched out
reaching for a dollar bill to light a single candle
for a wretched bishop
the virgin mary stands still all night
while the candle burns over and over
the young girls turn over on the sheets
behind a tree, behind the altar
in the confession box
where cardinal sin is masturbating his wealth
in a gold chalice of warped dreams
outliving the prostitutes and the poor
mayor gordon gives his pimp approval of
every young girl to be sold over the counter
turning every church into a whorehouse
the young dark pinays sing the songs they know best
i'll take romance
it's better to catch a sailor boy
and sail off to america
than to die in the philippines
falling in love again. . . i can't help it
what am i to do
falling in love with america is full time
the US sailor boys treat the young pinays
like part-time or half-time
a full-time brown lady is a waste of time
dancing on a silver dollar
dancing on a dime is prime time
the tagalog words flow from their mouths
like fish from the sea
mountain scales echo deep
in the lonely pit of sad dreams
teach me english, those english words like
fuck me or leave me
in the barrios with the olongapo pimps
isn't it romantic
etched on their brown faces

Tiao-yu Tai Islands

Tiao-yu Tai Island
stretches 20 nautical miles
from Taiwan & 240 miles from
Ryukyu (Okinawa)

Centuries past
Thousands of Chinese fishermen
made their living around the islands

And now America & Japan
drove the fishermen away
spilling oil
sinking their tongues
across the Islands and Seas

25 years lapsed by
and sharp Muromachi blades
sliced the Islands
in half

And the torn yellow flesh
of the War Resistance
is still alive

The blood soaked-up
Tiao-yu Tai Islands
Thick with wilted grasses
and reeds

Dead bones scattered
frozen still
Left over on jagged rocks.

Dark clouds overhead
No longer dead silence
Trees grow blood-red autumn
forever strong
Pounding hard
rising high.

Fresh as early spring fish
wiggling around
in broken jade brains.

The deep sea carved
the fisherman's life
and the Tiao-yu Tai winds
swept the mountains
of their minds clean
into a thousand rains.

Bitter is the winter rind
that spews forth sorrow
Soon lasting joy.

Rappin' with Ten Thousand Carabaos in the Dark

International Hotel—in the mongo heart & isda mind of the
Philippines—where old & young Pilipinos live, hang, &
roam around all day like carabaos in the mud: eating, sleep-
ing & working. Pilipinos scattered all over—brown faces piled
high, moving like shadows on trees, concrete doorways,
pool halls, barber shops. Guitar music echoes thru—
down deep in your mongo heart & isda mind. Chinatown
across the way. Sixty-thousand or more live in rooms the
size of tea pots, stretching east, west, north & south.
Thousands are crammed in damp basements, alley ways,
behind run-down barrels of ancient Chinese mountain wine.
Thousands of Chinese children run along soy sauce streets—
long black hair glistening like a cool stream—a quiet moon
watches. Short crop of hair—morning spring faces—
underneath fresh-soaked clouds. All those tiny footsteps
keep the winter belly warm.

All night session—ocean of words
Legaspi–Frank–Bob–Bill Sorro–Mee Har–Me
& somebody else.
Early start at Legaspi's UFA mountain fortress

Put down your white mind
with your eyes behind brown skin
brown=brown=brown=brown
fallen coconuts on a cold
cold winter day.
brown=brown=brown=brown
fish drying
in the hot summer sun.

Bill Sorro: "You know, when I go into the poolhalls
& see my Pilipino brothers, I want to say to them:

'You know I know how you feel; I know how you think.'
I want to say to them,
'Manong, manong, manong, don't you know
you are being fucked.'"

"I am brown, I am together, I am beautiful"
Come down from those white flaky hills
the smell of the carabao shit stills
the mind
keeps the pampano swimming
in your belly.
Put down your knives & forks
and eat rice & fish
with brown winter-soiled hands.
Jump and wallow
in the mountain-grass heap shit
of the carabao.

Ah, Pilipinos
if you only knew how brown you are
you would slide down
from the highest
mountain top
you would whip out your lava tongue
& burn up all that white shit
that's keeping your people down.

Don't you know
you smell like
the deep brown earth
if you only knew
if your eyes were
only opened
you would see the sun
come down

if you only knew
you would bring the sun down
on the grass
underneath brown children's feet.

You can't hide the fish heads
in your pockets
the smell is too strong.

But wait!
I'll whip out
a sharp bamboo leaf
and push it down
your throat
but I'll be gentle
I'll push it down
with my bolo
& you will cry out
maybe see into the dawn
hear water buffaloes
galloping along the river

Rain will fall
& wash your skin down
& you will tear off your clothes
listen to the strong wind
& you will run wild with your bolo
with your mind fired
with tons of burning lava
& you will feel the winter rain beat down
on your naked brown body
& you will be by the people
on the sand
by the water
in the mountains

& you will have your sharp bolo
& sing & dance
& eat & fight

All day into
the hot blazing sun
thru the cool dark night
onto the next morning
Behind the early morning fog
a million brown pilipino faces
chanting: makibaka, makibaka, makibaka
makibaka, makibaka, makibaka

Asian Center

Asian Center for the old—downstairs
in the basement—near the International
Hotel. Mr. Low cares for the old Chinese
Legaspi cares for the old pilipinos

two ancient chinese
standing in the center
like an orange egg yolk
in a lotus bun

"is Legaspi here?"

(a chinaman points his finger)

Legaspi sits quietly
silver-gray hair
ancient ifugao eyes
a spring sprig
pushed through
kearny street cries
young faces crowd
the pool halls

"we have to clean up
the philippines.
there has to be a revolution"

back alleys
loneliness
in cheap coffins
dead and forgotten
pilipinos
out of a finger

a widow bleeds
shield and sealed
in holy water
drowning primitive minds
wrapped in angelic garments
and metal crosses
break the eternal rituals
of the priest
pressing pilipino minds
into wailing fanatics

Yukio Mishima 48 Ronin

Sen No Rikyu
sipped his
last cup of koicha
then ended
his life

48 Ronin bowed
to the earth
then drove blades
sharper than
winter grass
into their bellies
silencing
shibui
sabi
wabi
furu
silencing
Basho's haiku
silencing
the four seasons
forever.

Yukio Mishima 48 Ronin
Set the cherry blossoms
to flame
when the autumn blade
touched the bottom
of his belly
& the blood
froze
as it touched
the cold wind

Yukio Mishima 48 Ronin
For whom? For what?
For whom? For what?
For your country?
that's still sitting
drinking tea
watching the quiet moon
while your body & mind
empty themselves into the ground.

Visiting the Grave of Edwardo Bedajos

Returning once more to Hawaii
Visiting a poet's grave
The drifting sand turns over my mind
How much does life offer the poet?
When nothing remains the same
Everything belongs to the wind
Searching for a poet's grave
With Jim, Tais & Jade
Stepping over gravestone after gravestone
"Over here!" Jade says. "Over here!" Tais says.
"Right here!" Jim says.
Row number thirteen
Standing on top of his grave
Listening to his silent words
Rising over mountains & hills
Fog & mist covered his whole mind
Traveled south together
Heading to Delano
Tadpoles croaked & crickets chirped
All night long
His guitar strings plucked feathers
From fighting cocks
How could I forget this poet?
Life was so precious to him
His poems rise up like wildfire

From the Poet's Place
(for russell leong)

in late november
chilled winds
surrounded by douglas fir
bells and gongs
fire and incense
books and poems
rice and tea
buddhist beads
knotted like one's mind
jagged mountains
of the buddha heart
ancient spirits moan
in wind and rain
fallen leaves
bringing back the mind
to all natural things
a moss grown mind
in the shade
gathering with friends
a book of poems
already collected dust
scattering them in the wind
shredding memories
strands of gray hair
a flight of birds
i hear sounds in the back woods
from the poet's place
there is a clear view
of Ten Worlds.

Photo by Chris Huie

International Hotel, Kearny Street

Ode to Bill Sorro

—poet

bill sorro
cried today
he cried
for his countryman
for a manong
from the philippines
who died
on his lap ·
in the children's playground
at portsmouth square
bill sorro
cried today
in his small room
at the international hotel
because
manong santos died
and juliana sat there
listening
to a voice
cut sharp
like a bolo
when he read his poem
to santos
who never had
a chance
to see his country again
bill sorro
cried for santos of the international hotel
santos of the st.paul hotel
santos of kearny street
santos of manilatown
santos his kababayan
santos of his brown hands
digging for his roots.

brings all themes together

Knowledge lost when people die

Photo by Alan Kikuchi

AL ROBLES was born in San Francisco, California, into a large family of twelve. He has lived practically his whole life in the Fillmore area. A poet, he has taught in the schools and prisons. Since the early 1970s, he has been a member of the Kearny Street Workshop. As a poet-oral historian for the San Francisco Art Commission under the CETA program, Robles has worked closely with the manongs collecting their histories and stories in Manilatown.